Eyes *that* Kiss in the Corners

By Joanna Ho
Illustrated by Dung Ho

HARPER
An Imprint of HarperCollinsPublishers

21 22 23 PC 10 9 8 7 6 5 4 3 2

❖

First Edition

For Aila. You are a revolution.
—J.H.

To my mama and my sisters.
—D.H.

Some people have
eyes like sapphire lagoons
with lashes like lace trim on ballgowns,
sweeping their cheeks as they twirl.
Big eyes, long lashes.

Not me.

I have eyes that kiss in the corners and glow like warm tea.

My eyes are just like Mama's.

Mama's eyes that kiss in the corners and glow like warm tea
crinkle into crescent moons

      when she comes home from work.

      She scoops me in her arms,

         eyes sparkling like starlight,

         and tickles me

         until we laugh ourselves onto the floor.

When Mama tucks me in at night, her eyes tell me
I'm a miracle.
In those moments when she's all mine,
flecks of dancing gold tell me
I'm hers too.

My Mama is my sun and sky,
and her eyes are just like Amah's.

Amah's eyes that kiss in the corners and glow like warm tea
don't work like they used to.
But she sees all the way into my heart
and can even read my mind.

Her eyes are filled with so many stories;
I can fall inside them
and swim until time stops.

I see
Guanyin with the Monkey King
sitting on a lotus, serene,

baubles of lychee on trees,
and mountains that reach for the sea.

My Amah never ages,
and her eyes are just like Mei-Mei's.

Mei-Mei's eyes that kiss in the corners and glow like warm tea
blink against the window until I come home from school.

They disappear
beneath her two-tooth smile
when I walk in the door.

She toddles after me,
gazing up at me
like I am her best present.
I hope she looks at me like that forever.
Because when she looks at me in that Mei-Mei way,
I feel like I can fly.

Mei-Mei's eyes that kiss in the corners and glow like warm tea
are just like mine.

My eyes crinkle into crescent moons
and sparkle like the stars.
Gold flecks dance and twirl
while stories whirl
in their oolong pools,
carrying tales of the past
and hope for the future.

My eyes find mountains
that rise ahead
and look up
when others shut down.

My lashes curve like the
swords of warriors
and, through them,
I see kingdoms in the clouds.

My eyes that kiss in the corners and
glow like warm tea
are a revolution.

They are Mama
         and Amah
         and Mei-Mei.

They are me.
And they are beautiful.